BIG, BAD
BARNEY BEAR

BIG, BAD
BARNEY BEAR

Written and illustrated by
TONY ROSS

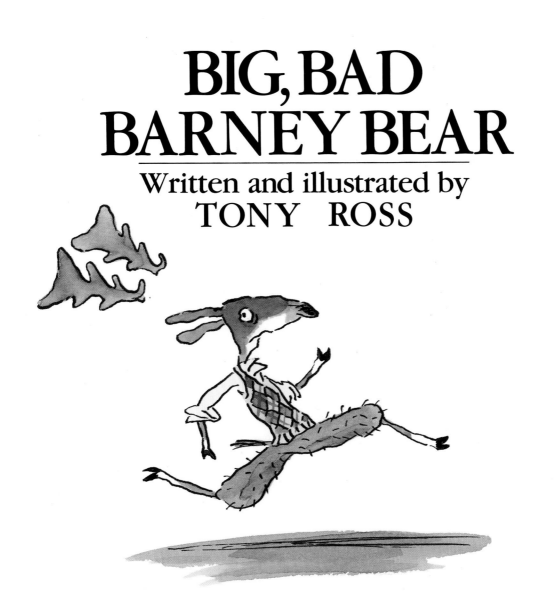

Red Fox

A Red Fox Book

Published by Random House Children's Books
20 Vauxhall Bridge Road, London SW1V 2SA

A division of Random House UK Ltd
London Melbourne Sydney Auckland
Johannesburg and agencies throughout the world

1 3 5 7 9 10 8 6 4 2

First published in Great Britain by Andersen Press 1992

Red Fox edition 1994

Printed in Hong Kong

RANDOM HOUSE UK Limited Reg. No. 954009

ISBN 0 09 927221 0

Moose was bored, so he decided to go and find a job.

He found lots of work on the building site.

One shovel looked better than the others...

...so Moose chose it for himself.

Moose was not happy, but he started work.

He worked hard for an hour, until it was time for coffee.

Moose chose the cup that would hold the most coffee, but he had to take a smaller one.

Moose was not happy. He took his small cup of coffee and settled in a large comfy chair...

...but he had to move onto an uncomfortable pile of bricks.

Moose was not happy, he could take no more...

...and the other animals trembled.

The crocodile pointed to a factory that
BIG BAD BARNEY BEAR had built...

...but Moose was not impressed.
He wanted to find the bear...

...and put him in his place...

...once and for all!

At daybreak, Moose came across a lonely cottage, big enough for a bear.

He knocked on the door, and it was opened by a huge animal.

With a roar, Moose charged. Skin and teeth flew, fur and trouser buttons…

...until at last, Moose was the winner.

The bear was bruised, and baffled.

and didn't seem to understand...

...why.

Some
bestselling Red Fox
picture books

THE BIG ALFIE AND ANNIE ROSE STORYBOOK
by Shirley Hughes
OLD BEAR
by Jane Hissey
OI! GET OFF OUR TRAIN
by John Burningham
DON'T DO THAT!
by Tony Ross
NOT NOW, BERNARD
by David McKee
ALL JOIN IN
by Quentin Blake
THE WHALES' SONG
by Gary Blythe and Dyan Sheldon
JESUS' CHRISTMAS PARTY
by Nicholas Allan
THE PATCHWORK CAT
by Nicola Bayley and William Mayne
MATILDA
by Hilaire Belloc and Posy Simmonds
WILLY AND HUGH
by Anthony Browne
THE WINTER HEDGEHOG
by Ann and Reg Cartwright
A DARK, DARK TALE
by Ruth Brown
HARRY, THE DIRTY DOG
by Gene Zion and Margaret Bloy Graham
DR XARGLE'S BOOK OF EARTHLETS
by Jeanne Willis and Tony Ross
WHERE'S THE BABY?
by Pat Hutchins